For Eirann Grace, T. Rex's original pen pal
—L.M.

For Angelina
—J.M.

Library of Congress Cataloging-in-Publication Data
McClatchy, Lisa.
Dear Tyrannosaurus Rex / by Lisa McClatchy ; illustrations by John Manders.
p. cm.
Summary: Enamored of dinosaurs, Erin writes a letter inviting a real one to her sixth birthday party.
ISBN 978-0-375-85608-2 (trade) — ISBN 978-0-375-95608-9 (lib. bdg.)
[1. Tyrannosaurus rex—Fiction. 2. Dinosaurs—Fiction. 3. Parties—Fiction. 4. Birthdays—Fiction.]
I. Manders, John, ill. II. Title.
PZ7.M47841375De 2010
[E]—dc22   2009005038

MANUFACTURED IN CHINA
10 9 8 7 6 5 4 3 2 1
First Edition

Dear TYRANNOSAURUS REX

by Lisa McClatchy

illustrated by John Manders

Random House 🏠 New York

As her sixth birthday drew near, Erin decided that it was high time to invite a REAL dinosaur to her birthday party. So she pulled out a piece of paper and her favorite dinosaur pen and began....

Dear Tyrannosaurus Rex,

I am turning 6 in two weeks. Please come to my birthday party! I know your museum is far, far away, but it would mean the world to me if you could make it!

I have enclosed a map to my house so you won't get lost.

When you get to my street, there will be big red balloons and signs to show you the way.

If you come to my party, my family and friends will greet you on the front porch.

(Don't let Violet scare you! She just has a really big bark!)

If you come to my party, we'll set up a big tent in the backyard—in case it rains. Remember to duck!

There will be lots of party favors....
We'll have dinosaur hats
and dinosaur horns
and toys that look just like you!

If you come to my party, we'll play pirates on my play set! Your tail will make a great slide!

If you come to my party,
we'll play pin the tail on the
dinosaur…

and hide-and-seek …

and TWISTER,
your favorite!

If you come to my party, we'll teach you
duck, duck, goose and musical chairs!

If you come to my party, we'll do the hokey-pokey and turn ourselves around … and we'll jump on the trampoline.

If you come to my party, we'll order pepperoni pizzas, since I know you are a meat-eater. I guess we'll need a lot of them!

If you come to my party, I'll let you take the first whack at the piñata!!

If you come to my party, my mom will bake an extra-large birthday cake! You can help me blow out the candles.

If you come to my party, you can help me open my presents!

If you come to my party, we'll have pony rides!
Or maybe we could ride on your back instead?

If you come to my party, you'll get a goody bag for your trip home! If there are any left over, you can take them back to your friends.

If you come to my party, I'll be the happiest girl in the world.

Please come to my party.

Love,
Erin

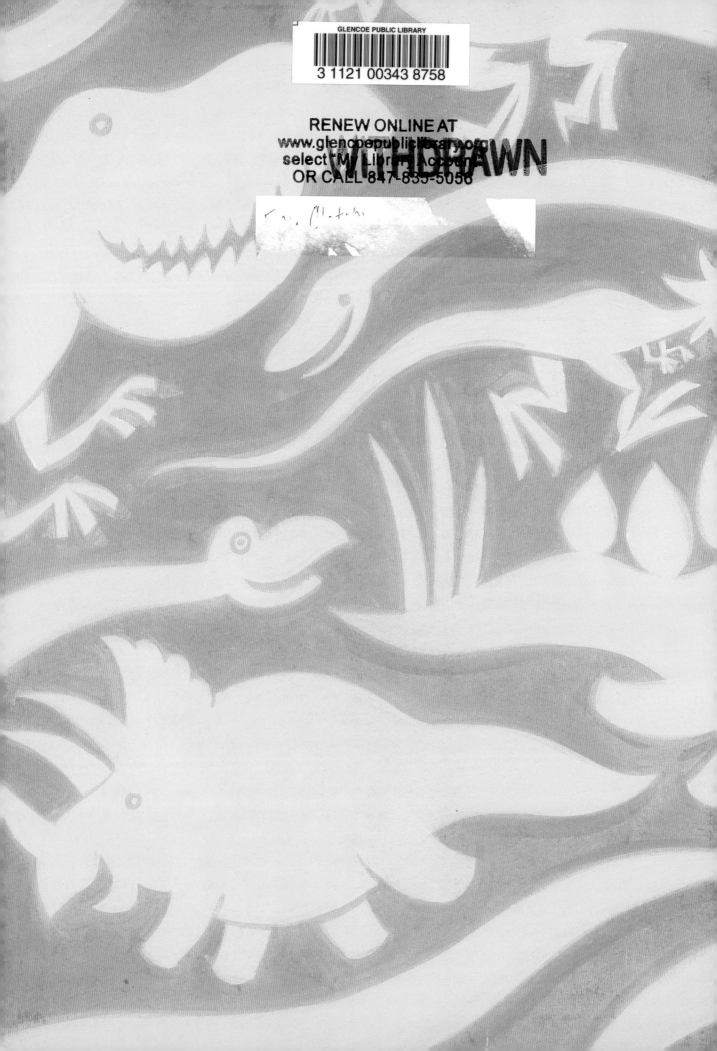